Dear Katie,
The Volcano *IS* a Girl

Jean Craighead George

Illustrated by Daniel Powers

Hyperion Books for Children

New York

To my granddaughter Katie—JCG

In honor of Pele and her creative fire in each of us.
Thanks to The Kalani Honua Institute for making the
research for *Dear Katie, The Volcano IS a Girl* possible.—DTP

$\mathcal{K}$atie and her grandmother stood on a hillside in Hawaii watching the Kilauea Volcano erupt. Fires lit up its sloping cone. Lightning flashed about it. The wind screamed. Hot orange-red lava glowed along its side. When it rolled into the sea it exploded into sizzling fireworks.

"A volcano is a geophysical phenomenon," the grandmother said grandly.

"The volcano is a girl," said Katie.

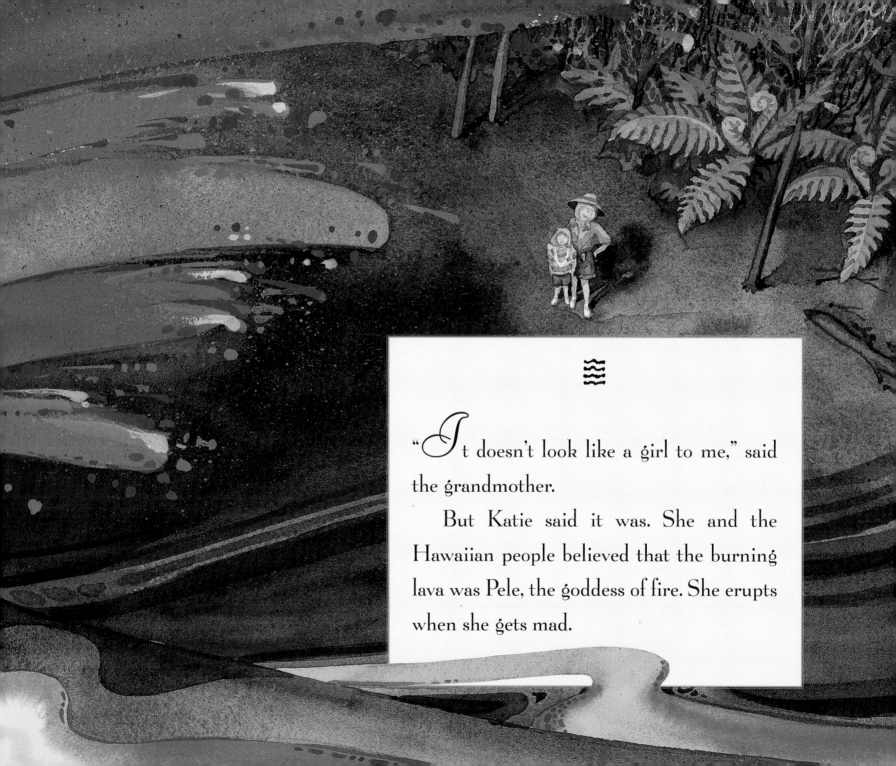

"It doesn't look like a girl to me," said the grandmother.

But Katie said it was. She and the Hawaiian people believed that the burning lava was Pele, the goddess of fire. She erupts when she gets mad.

"No," said the grandmother. "Long ago rocky pieces of the ocean floor sank into the fiery core of the earth. There they heated into rising lava blobs. The lava found weak spots on the ocean floor and burst free."

"Pele burst free," Katie corrected.

The grandmother continued. "The lava fell on the ocean floor, and piled up until it was above the surface of the water. The Hawaiian Islands were born. Lava makes this land."

"Pele makes this land," said Katie.

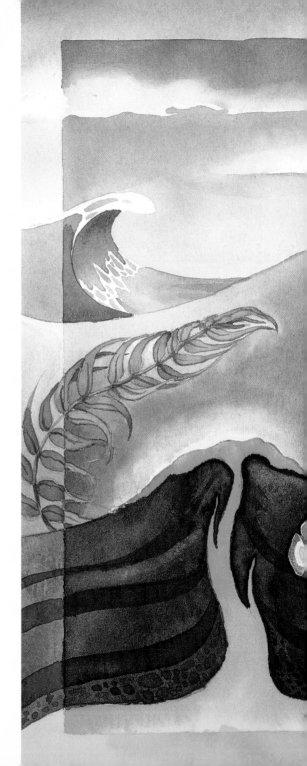

They looked down on the site of a town. It was buried under ten feet of cold lava. On that eerie black landscape, only the roof of a school bus and a street light told where the town had been. Lava creeps slowly, about three feet an hour. The people had walked away from their homes, promising to come back and rebuild the town.

The grandmother said the people coming home would be the epilogue to an eruption. "There is also a prelude," she said.

Before a volcanic eruption violent earthquakes crack open the ocean floor. The earthquakes create gargantuan tidal waves. The tidal waves crash down on the land and carry away cliffs, beaches, and mountainsides.

Katie told the story that the Hawaiians tell. "The tidal waves are Pele's older sister, Na Maka o Kaha'i, the goddess of the sea. She is jealous of Pele. She becomes a huge tidal wave and chases Pele off every island she has ever lived on—all except Hawaii and Maui. Pele lives on Hawaii in Kilauea Volcano and she is mad at her sister right now."

"The truth is," the grandmother said, "the earth's crust is a jigsaw of huge sliding pieces called plates. They have been drifting on top of the molten inner earth for billions of years. One plate is carrying the Hawaiian Islands away from the spot where the lava erupts."

"Where Pele erupts," Katie corrected.

"Where the lava erupts," the grandmother recorrected. "When an island is carried away from the hot spot, it cools down," explained the grandmother. "A fern takes hold, then a flower. A forest is born. People arrive. Back on the floor of the ocean the hot spot erupts again and a new island begins."

". . . when Pele gets mad at her sister," Katie finished.

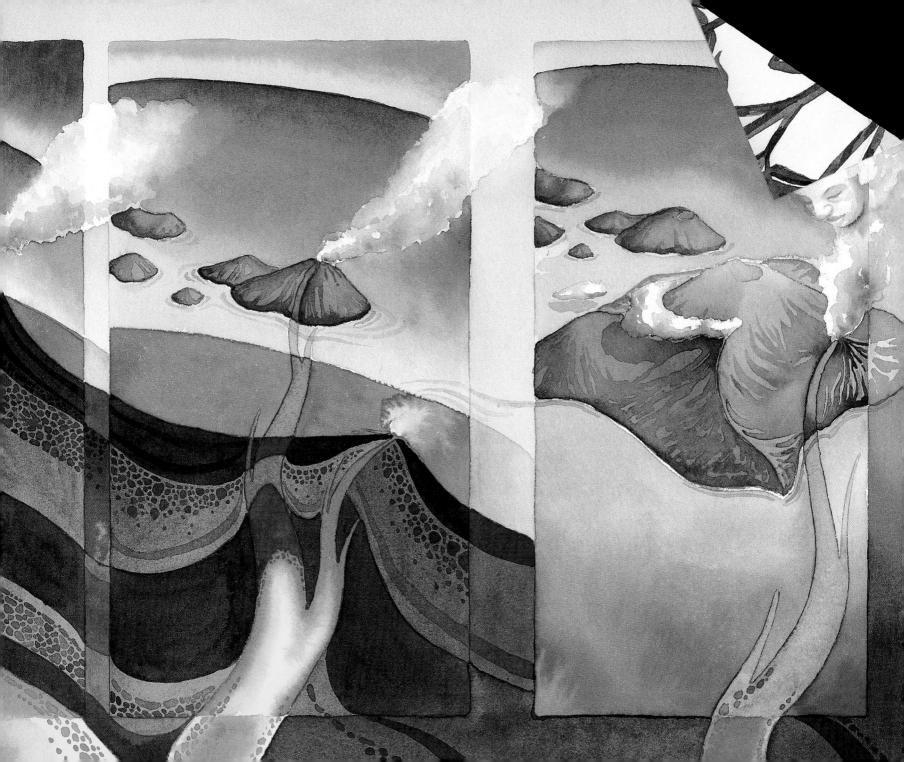

They journeyed to the other side of Kilauea, a volcano so big that it was erupting on one side and quiet on the other. It is the world's largest erupting volcano.

Iki, a volcano within Kilauea crater, had erupted a few years ago. The Hawaiian volcanoes do not explode like Mount Etna and Mount Saint Helens did. They ooze fiery lava, and then they die down.

It was quiet. The grandmother started down the trail to the bottom of the crater. Katie hesitated.

"This is Pele's home," she said. "She hasn't invited us to walk over it."

The grandmother smiled and took Katie's hand.

They made their way downward through the dark ferns, ohi'a and koa trees. Bright sunlight filled the bottom of the crater. Black walls rose around them like a stone casket. They were inside the volcano crater. Echoes moaned off walls.

"A volcano eruption is a killer," said the grandmother looking around. "I hear no birds. I see no scurrying beasts."

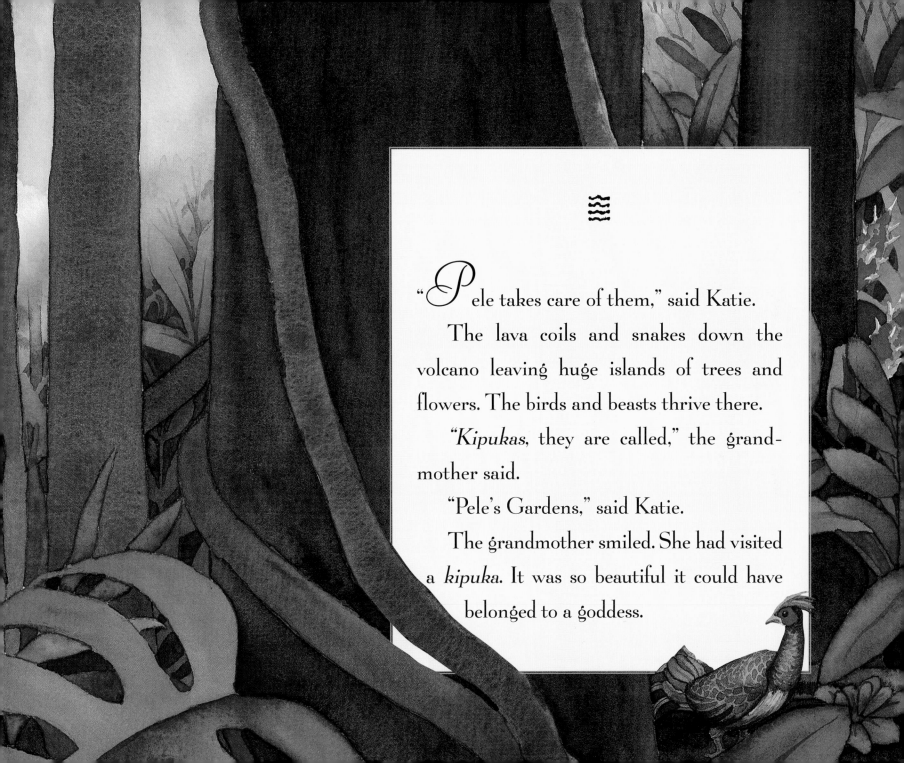

≋

"Pele takes care of them," said Katie.

The lava coils and snakes down the volcano leaving huge islands of trees and flowers. The birds and beasts thrive there.

"*Kipukas*, they are called," the grandmother said.

"Pele's Gardens," said Katie.

The grandmother smiled. She had visited a *kipuka*. It was so beautiful it could have belonged to a goddess.

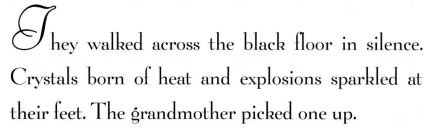They walked across the black floor in silence. Crystals born of heat and explosions sparkled at their feet. The grandmother picked one up.

"Put it down, Grammy," Katie said. "That's one of Pele's tears."

The grandmother put it down.

Threads as golden as Katie's hair were laced across the crater floor. Katie held one in the sun.

The threads form when the lava blows into the sky. The sand from the lava cools and spins silicon threads.

"This is Pele's hair," said Katie. She held it up.

"It does look like hair," the grandmother said.

$\approx$

Quietly Katie got down on her hands and knees. She put her ear against the lava and listened. What was she listening to? To the earth's crust that sunk eons ago and was now coming back to the surface? To other voices?

"What do you hear?" the grandmother finally asked.

"Pele," Katie answered. "She said it's all right for us to walk across her home."

"That's very nice of Pele."

Katie looked at her grandmother in open surprise. "You called her Pele."

"Well, that's her name isn't, it?"

So that's how it happened, Katie. You told me the beautiful legend. I told you the scientist's story and they were the same.

Love,
Grammy XX

Printed in the United States of America.
First Edition
1 3 5 7 9 10 8 6 4 2

The artwork for this book was prepared using watercolor paint.
This book is set in 17-point BeLucian Book.
Designed by Stephanie Bart-Horvath.

Library of Congress Cataloging-in-Publication Data
George, Jean Craighead.
Dear Katie, The Volcano IS a Girl / Jean Craighead George ; illustrated by
Daniel Powers.—1st ed.
p.   cm.
Summary: A grandmother and her granddaughter argue over
whether a volcano is a geophysical phenomenon or an angry Hawaiian goddess.
ISBN 0-7868-0314-2 (trade)   ISBN 0-7868-2254-6 (lib. bdg.)
[1. Volcanoes—Fiction. 2. Kilauea Volcano (Hawaii)—Fiction.
3. Pele (Hawaiian deity)—Fiction. 4. Grandmothers—Fiction.
5. Hawaii—Fiction.] I. Powers, Daniel, ill. II. Title.
PZ7.G2933Vo 1998
[Fic]-dc21   97-38885